dead in bed

Sweetfern Harbor Cozy Mystery - 2

wendy meadows

MAJESTIC OWL PUBLISHING LLC

Majestic Owl Publishing LLC
P.O. Box 997
Newport, NH 03773

Created with Vellum

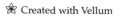